Papa Bear's
PAGE FRIGHT

BY WADE BRADFORD

ILLUSTRATED BY MARY ANN FRASER

PB Peter Pauper Press, Inc.
WHITE PLAINS, NEW YORK

First edition 2018

Published by Peter Pauper Press, Inc.

202 Mamaroneck Avenue

White Plains, New York 10601 USA

Published in the United Kingdom and Europe by Peter Pauper Press, Inc.

c/o White Pebble International

Unit 2, Plot 11 Terminus Rd.

Chichester, West Sussex PO19 8TX, UK

Library of Congress Cataloging-in-Publication Data

Names: Bradford, Wade, author. | Fraser, Mary Ann, illustrator.

Title: Papa Bear's Page Fright / by Wade Bradford ; illustrated by Mary Ann Fraser.

Description: First edition. | White Plains, New York : Peter Pauper Press, Inc., 2018. | Summary: As a narrator begins telling the story of Goldilocks and the Three Bears, Papa develops Page Fright, is unable to say his lines, and runs away through other books.

Identifiers: LCCN 2017037275 | ISBN 9781441325983 (hardcover : alk. paper)

Subjects: | CYAC: Stage fright--Fiction. | Bears--Fiction. | Characters in literature--Fiction. | Humorous stories.

Classification: LCC PZ7.B7229 Pap 2018 | DDC [E]--dc23 LC record available at https://lccn.loc.gov/2017037275

ISBN 978-1-4413-2598-3

Manufactured for Peter Pauper Press, Inc.

Printed in Hong Kong

7 6 5 4 3 2 1

Visit us at www.peterpauper.com

TO ATHAN, HUDSON, AND BAILEY

– W.B.

FOR ALLISON

– M.A.F.

This is the story of a little girl named Goldilocks.

Hello! Welcome to my story.

She loved to explore
the great outdoors.

Little did she know that in the middle of the forest there was a cozy little cabin, and inside the cozy little cabin lived three bears.

Mama Bear.

Baby Bear.

And Papa Bear said . . .

SMASH!

hare stopped for a rest in the shade
tree, but the tortoise, slow and steady,
continued on toward the finish line.

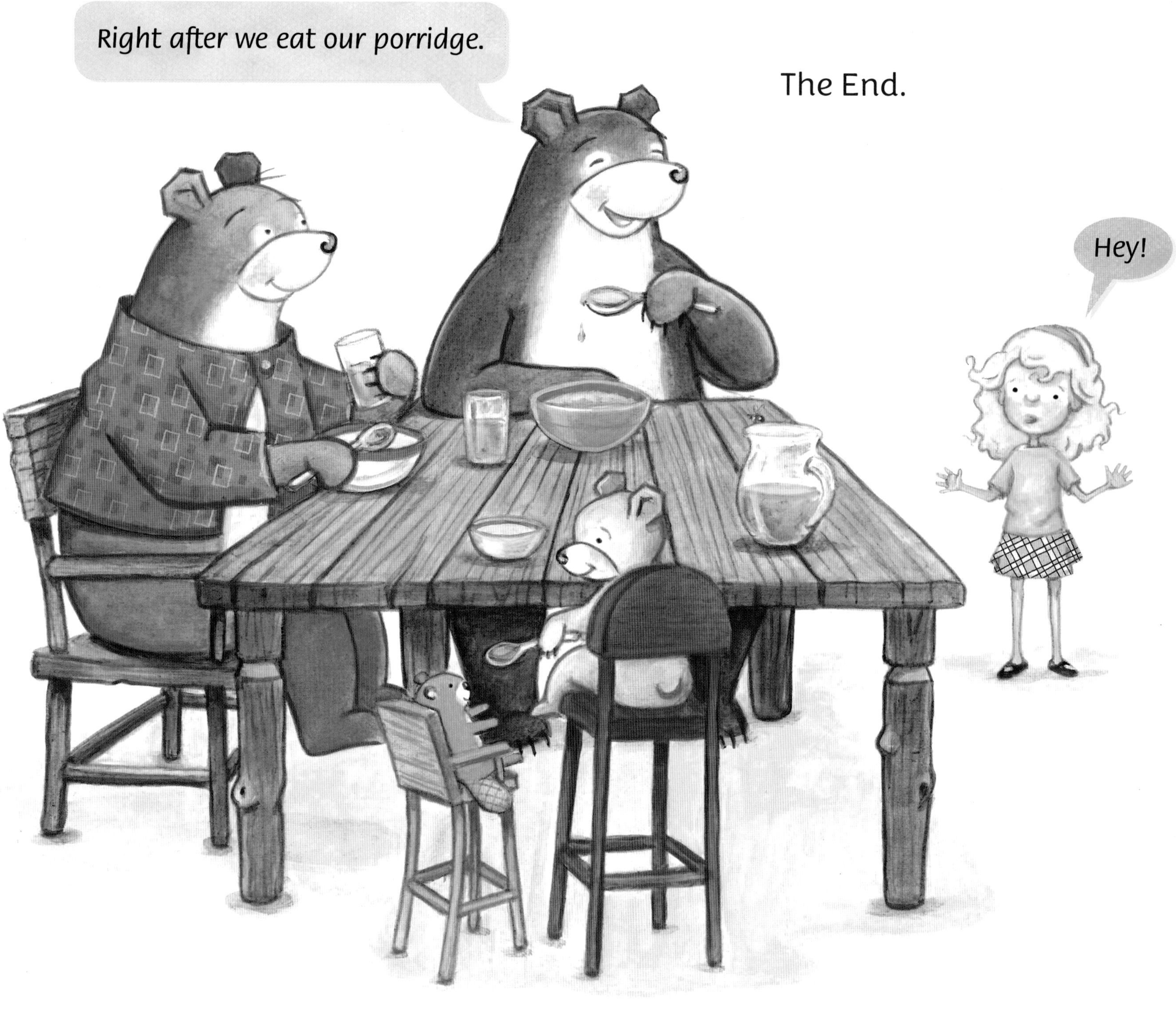

The End.